Peter Rabbit's
Words, Colors
and
Numbers

Based on the original tales
BY BEATRIX POTTER

F. WARNE & Cº

animal friends

butterfly

hen

chick

duck

duckling

kitten

cat

cows

mouse

dog

Which animal friend do you like best?

hedgehog

bird

rabbit

frog

fish

tortoise

snail

worm

pig

fox

rat

things we do

Mrs Tiggy-winkle is always busy. Look at her doing the **ironing**.
Everyone else here is doing something too.
Can you do all of these things?

Mrs Tittlemouse
is **sweeping** up
the dust

Mrs Tiggy-winkle is doing the **ironing**

Anna Maria is
rolling out the dough

Mrs Rabbit
is **going**
shopping

Peter is **standing** up straight

Mr McGregor is **chasing** Peter Rabbit

Pigling Bland and Alexander are **dancing**

Jemima Puddle-duck is **flying**

Benjamin Bunny is **sitting** down

Peter is **pointing** at Benjamin Bunny

The foxy gentleman is **reading** a newspaper. Everyone else here is doing something too.
Can you do all of these things?

Mrs Tabitha Twitchit is **brushing** her kittens

The mouse is **drinking** from a glass

The kittens are **playing** together

Mrs Tittlemouse is **sleeping** in her rocking chair

Mr Jeremy
Fisher is **putting
on** his shoes

Mr Jeremy
Fisher is
hopping
to the
pond

Mr Jeremy Fisher is
digging for worms

Sam Whiskers
is **tiptoeing**

Mr Jeremy
Fisher is
fishing

Pig-wig is
eating
oatmeal

Anna Maria is
carrying her
bundles

clothes

coat

necktie

vest

pants

boots

Tommy Brock is a short, bristly, fat, waddling person with a grin all over his face. He eats wasps' nests and frogs and worms; and he waddles about by moonlight, digging things up. His clothes are very dirty, and as he sleeps in the day-time, he always goes to bed in his boots!

bonnet

dress

blouse

apron

petticoat

Mrs Tiggy-winkle is a very stout, short person who is rather shy and anxious. She wears her dress tucked in to do the ironing, and she has a large apron over her striped petticoat. Her little black nose goes sniffle, sniffle, snuffle, and her eyes go twinkle, twinkle. Can you see the prickles underneath her bonnet?

blue

ball of yarn

flowers

policeman's
uniform

Peter Rabbit's
jacket

Pig-wig's
dress

Tom Kitten's suit button

Anna Maria's
dress

Peter Rabbit wears a blue jacket.
Everyone on this page is wearing something blue.
Do you have any blue clothes?

yellow

stockings

ducklings

duck's feet and beak

gentleman mouse's jacket

lady mouse's dress

chick

Samuel Whiskers' vest and pants

What color are the ducklings?
Can you point to all the yellow things on this page?

 green

door

John Joiner's
jacket

Aunt Pettitoes'
apron

plants

Mr Tod's
suit

What color is Aunt Pettitoes' apron?
Point to all the green things on this page.
Who can you see behind the green door?

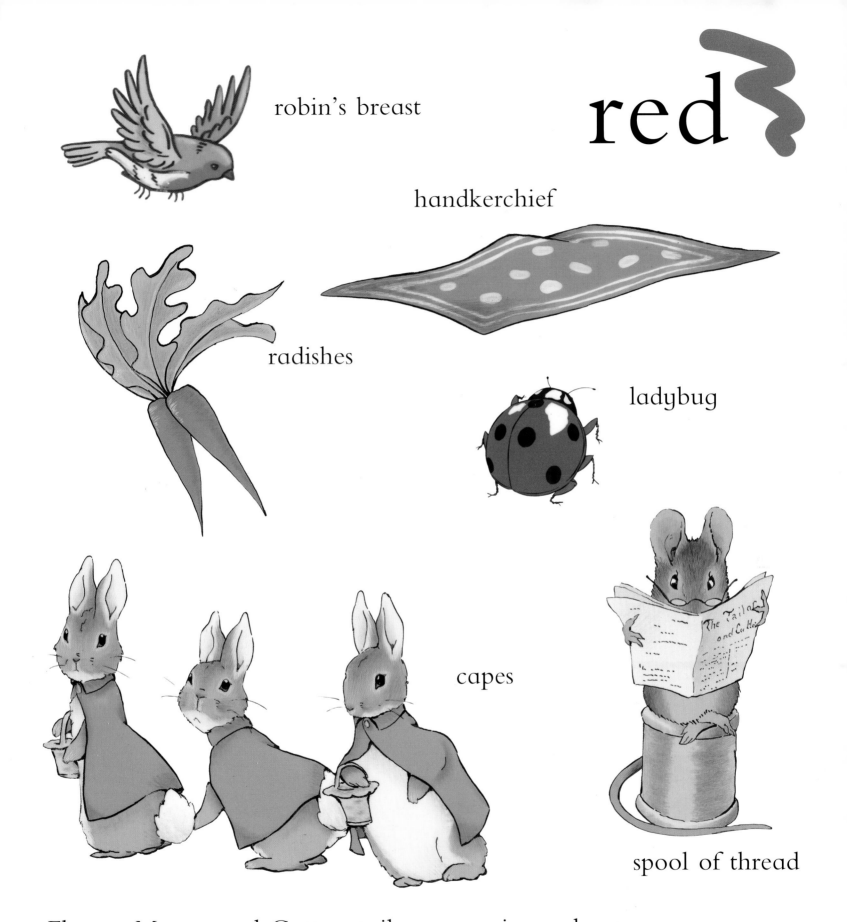

robin's breast

red

handkerchief

radishes

ladybug

capes

spool of thread

Flopsy, Mopsy and Cotton-tail are wearing red capes.
Point to the red ladybug. Now you can point to all the red
things on this page!

black

beetle

birds

Sir Isaac Newton's pants

cat

duck

eggs

pitcher

Mittens' and Moppet's dresses

white

Mrs Tabitha Twitchit's dress

purple

Hunca Munca's dress

Mr Bouncer's coat

flower

pants on the washing line

Pigling Bland's jacket

Flopsy Bunny

Samuel Whiskers' bag

brown

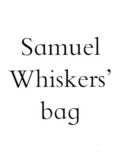

numbers

1 One duck, her name is Jemima Puddle-duck

2 Two naughty rabbits, named Peter and Benjamin

3 One, two, three kittens named Mittens, Tom Kitten and Moppet

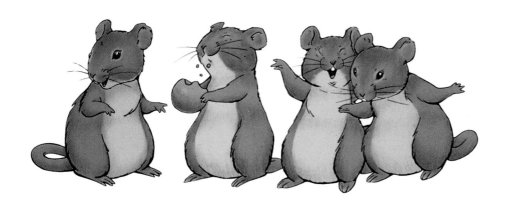

4 Four giggling mice

5 Five juicy heads of lettuce for Peter Rabbit

6 Six hens, clucking

7 Seven butterflies, fluttering

8 Eight mice, all dressed up

9

Nine eggs,
freshly laid

10

Ten bumble bees,
buzzing

in the kitchen

How many plates can you see on the dresser?

How many drawers can you count?

What color is Mrs Tiggy-winkle's bonnet?

What color are the pants hanging on the washing line?

Point to the stool.

Can you find these objects in the picture?

kettle and saucepan

basket

pitcher

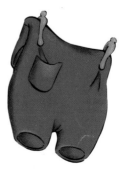

pants

iron

how many?

Can you count the onions?

How many bags and parcels, for Anna Maria?

How many rabbit-babies is Flopsy holding?

How many radishes is Peter holding?

How many cats on the basket?

How many peas is the mouse carrying?

what color?

Do you recognize the colors of all these clothes?

Tommy Brock's necktie

Jemima Puddle-duck's bonnet

Mrs Tittlemouse's petticoat

Mr Jackson's coat

Johnny Town-mouse's vest and pants

Tom Kitten's shirt and pants

Alexander's jacket

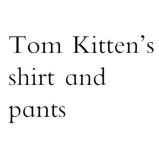

FREDERICK WARNE

Published by the Penguin Group
27 Wrights Lane, London W8 5TZ, England
Penguin Books USA Inc., 375 Hudson Street, New York, New York 10014, USA
Penguin Books Australia Ltd, Ringwood, Victoria, Australia
Penguin Books Canada Ltd, 10 Alcorn Avenue, Toronto, Ontario, Canada M4V 3B2
Penguin Books (N.Z.) Ltd, 182-190 Wairau Road, Auckland 10, New Zealand

Penguin Books Ltd, Registered Offices: Harmondsworth, Middlesex, England

First published 1996 by Frederick Warne

3 5 7 9 10 8 6 4 2

ISBN 07232 4264X

Colour reproduction by Saxon Photolitho Ltd., Norwich
Printed and bound in Singapore by Tien Wah Press (Pte) Ltd